SYDNEY & TAYLOR

EXPLORE the WHOLE Wide WORLD

JACQUELINE DAVIES

Illustrated by DEBORAH HOCKING

Clarion Books
An imprint of HarperCollin Publishers
Boston New York

Text copyright © 2021 by Jacqueline Davies
Illustrations copyright © 2021 by Deborah Hocking

clarionbooks.com

The illustrations were done in gouache and colored pencil on watercolor paper,
with digital editing.
The text type was set in Plantin Std.
The display type was set in YWFT Absent Grotesque.

The Library of Congress Cataloging-in-Publication data is on file.
ISBN: 978-0-358-10631-9 paper over board
ISBN: 978-0-358-53166-1 paperback

Manufactured in Canada
FSE 10 9 8 7 6 5 4 3 2

To explorers everywhere, those who are afraid
and those who are not —J.D.

For my always wise and gracious big sister.
Love you, Shell! —D.H.

Chapter 1

Taylor is a hedgehog who lives with his friend Sydney in a burrow under Miss Nancy's potting shed.

Sydney, being a skunk, likes to nap in the burrow. He likes to warm his feet by the fire. He likes to listen to the strong, steady heartbeat of the earth, which you can only hear underground.

Taylor likes those things, too. But sometimes Taylor gets ideas. Big Ideas!

"Sydney," said Taylor one morning, "I have a Big Idea! We should go somewhere!"

"Why?" asked Sydney. "Our burrow is perfectly perfect."

"Yes, it is," said Taylor. "But wouldn't it be *exciting* to go someplace new?"

"Old is better than new," said Sydney. "And exciting is . . . exhausting."

Taylor sighed. "You are a very contented skunk. But I would like to see more of the Whole Wide World."

Sydney wanted his friend to be happy. "Well," he said, putting down his book. "Then we will."

Chapter 2

"We will launch an expedition," said Sydney.

"An expe-*what?*" asked Taylor.

"An expedition!" said Sydney.

Sydney began to open closets and empty drawers with great speed.

Taylor began to clutch his paws with great nervousness.

"Will we see new places?" asked Taylor.

"Absolutely!" said Sydney.

"Will we try new things?" asked Taylor.

"Without a doubt!" said Sydney.

"Will we meet . . . *strangers?*" asked Taylor.

"Tons of 'em," said Sydney.

"Oh," said Taylor, looking down at his paws. "Strangers." Taylor was afraid of strangers. He knew so few of them. Suddenly his Big Idea seemed like a scary idea.

"We will explore Places Unknown!" said Sydney. "Just what you've always wanted."

And then Taylor remembered. It *was* what he wanted! Even if he was afraid.

He ran upstairs and took down the map of the Whole Wide World. The map was Taylor's most prized possession.

"I'll plan the route," Taylor shouted to Sydney. "We are going on an expedition!"

Chapter 3

"It is an awful lot, isn't it?" said Taylor.

"There is absolutely no way we can carry all this," said Sydney.

"But it's an expedition," said Taylor. "To Places Unknown."

"Yes," said Sydney, "but not to Places on Mars!"

"I guess we don't need *all* the food," said Taylor.

"We have excellent noses. We can sniff out food along the way," said Sydney.

"And I guess we don't need *all* the water," said Taylor.

"We have excellent hearing. We can listen for streams along the way," said Sydney.

Taylor pulled a baseball bat from the pile.

"But we do need *this!*" he said.

"What for?" asked Sydney, taking the bat.

"In case we meet ferocious predators," said Taylor.

Sydney swished his tail back and forth. "If we meet ferocious predators, *they* will be the ones who will be sorry."

"What if . . . what if . . . what if we meet . . . Miss Nancy?" asked Taylor, shivering.

Sydney thought carefully.

They had never actually met Miss Nancy, although they had peeked at her from under the potting shed. And, of course, they knew her scent very well.

They had also never traveled beyond the fence that surrounded Miss Nancy's yard. Who knew what lay on the other side?

The Whole Wide World, that's what!

Mountains taller than a hundred hedgehogs.
Valleys wider than a thousand skunks. Forests
and rivers and caves.

They wanted to see it all! Taylor and Sydney
were feeling wild and fearless and free.

"If we meet Miss Nancy," said Sydney, pausing, "we'll simply hide behind a rock until she passes. Now, out we go!"

So with only a small pack on his back and nothing more than the map of the Whole Wide World in his tiny paws, Taylor stepped out into the dazzling sunlight.

Chapter 4

"I can't see! I can't see!" squealed Taylor in the bright sunshine.

"Don't panic!" said Sydney. "You always panic."

"I do not!" said Taylor, panicking.

He had dropped the map.

He had lost all sense of direction.

Even his nose was confused.

"Here," said Sydney, reaching into his satchel.

He handed Taylor a pair of sunglasses. Sydney put on a pair, too.

"This is much better," said Taylor.

"Good," said Sydney. "Ready to go?"

"Yes!" said Taylor. "Yes! Yes!"

Taylor picked up the map of the Whole Wide World and traced a path with his paw.

"We will head for the Little Stream. Then we will follow the Little Stream to the Old Footbridge. Then we will cross the Old Footbridge and be in the Great Meadow."

"That's awfully far, Taylor," said Sydney.

"Of course! It's an expedition!" said Taylor, marching off in the direction of the Little Stream.

"I suppose," sighed Sydney. He was already thinking of their cozy burrow and how nice it would be to take a nap.

But he followed his friend.

Chapter 5

Taylor and Sydney climbed over walls. They scampered up hills. They dug tunnels under hedges.

They lifted their noses to smell for danger. They kept their ears open to listen for ferocious predators.

But despite their hard work,

they didn't seem to travel very far

from Miss Nancy's house.

Still, they kept on.

"I just don't understand," said Taylor, stopping to look at the map. "From our burrow to the Old Footbridge is only this far." He held up his paws to show the distance. "I know we've walked farther than *that*."

"Taylor," said Sydney. "Just because it's that far on the map doesn't mean it's that far in the real world. Maps and the real world are different."

"They are?" asked Taylor. "Then what good is a map?"

"It gives a general sense of direction," said Sydney. "That's all you can ask of a map."

Taylor sighed. "I had expected more."

"Do you even know where we are?" asked Sydney.

Taylor shook his head. "We are hopelessly lost!"

It was true.

Nothing looked familiar.

Nothing sounded familiar.

Nothing smelled familiar.

Slowly, Taylor could feel his spine begin to bend. Hedgehogs curl up into a spiky ball when they are frightened.

"None of that!" said Sydney firmly. "This is our expedition. And these are Places Unknown. Just what we wanted! Come on!"

Sydney walked off quickly.

Taylor straightened his spine and scrambled to catch up.

Chapter 6

"Is this the part of the expedition where we stop to eat?" asked Taylor a few minutes later.

"Absolutely!" said Sydney. "Let's each have a tuna fish sandwich and some cheese, and then we'll be on our way." He sat down expectantly.

Taylor looked at Sydney and blinked in the bright sunshine. "But you told me not to bring any food," he said.

"I didn't say *any*," said Sydney. "I said *all*."

"Oh," said Taylor. "I must have mixed up the two."

"What have you got in your backpack, then?" asked Sydney.

"Mosquito repellant," said Taylor. "And sunscreen."

Sydney frowned. "You left *all* the food behind?"

"Every crumb!" said Taylor. "Every crust. Every carrot. Every pot of pudding."

"There was pudding?" asked Sydney.

"Chocolate with little bits of marshmallow," wailed Taylor.

"Well," said Sydney after a long pause.

"We will hunt for our dinner."

Hunt! Taylor couldn't remember the last time they had *hunted* for food. They always rummaged their supper out of Miss Nancy's garbage can.

"After all," said Sydney cheerfully. "This is an expedition. We will hunt like the wild animals we are."

"Yes!" said Taylor bravely, shivering with fright. "We are wild animals!"

Chapter 7

Taylor and Sydney crept along the edge of a road.

They kept their noses lifted to catch any scent.

When they heard water nearby, they left the road and scrambled to the top of a small hill. At the bottom of the hill was a stream.

Sydney and Taylor looked at the rushing water.

"Frogs!" whispered Sydney. "Go get 'em!"

"Me?" asked Taylor. "Why me?"

"Because you're the one who left the food at home," said Sydney.

Taylor sighed.

He waddled down the steep slope to the water's edge, where an army of frogs was gathered.

"Excuse me," said Taylor. He was shy around strangers. "I hate to bother you, but ... well, I'm not quite sure how to do this."

"What are you trying to do?" asked one of the frogs. She was shiny and green, with eyes the size of marbles.

"Hunt!" said Taylor proudly.

"Hunt what?" asked another frog.

"Well . . . *you*," said Taylor, who was a very honest hedgehog.

The frogs began to laugh. One of them laughed so hard he fell off his rock.

"If I were you," said one of the frogs, "I would worry less about hunting and more about *being* hunted." She pointed up the hill.

And with that, all the frogs dove underwater.

Taylor looked up the hill.

Chapter 8

"Yipes!" shouted Taylor.

An enormous dog was running his way.

Taylor could hear her ferocious barking.

He could smell her dangerous scent.

He could see the slobber hanging from her lips.

Snap!

Taylor curled into a spiky ball.

The ball rolled into the water and began to float downstream.

The dog reached the water's edge and barked loudly. She paced back and forth, ready to leap in.

Just then, Sydney strolled out from under a bush.

"Well, hello there!" said Sydney, swishing his tail back and forth. "Mighty fine day, wouldn't you say?"

The giant dog stopped barking. She couldn't understand Sydney's words. Dogs had lost their wildness by living with humans. They could no longer speak the language of the wild.

Still, they could be fierce.

Sydney advanced slowly, putting himself between the dog and the water.

His tail waved like a warning flag.

The dog backed up the hill. She let out a sharp " YAP! "

"I would say it's time you headed home," said Sydney sternly.

The dog was confused. But she knew that she wanted the spiky ball floating in the water.

She barked loudly and rushed straight at Sydney.

Chapter 9

In a flash, Sydney turned himself around, lifted his tail, and squirted a stream of stinky musk.

The dog yowled and ran away, whimpering.

"And *that's* how a skunk gets the job done," said Sydney.

"Hey, Stripe!" shouted a frog who had peeped up from underwater to watch the show. "Your friend floated away. You better hurry, or you'll never see him again!"

Sydney scuffled along the edge of the water as fast as he could.

He lifted his nose to catch the familiar scent of his old friend.

And there, after a few minutes, he spotted Taylor tangled in the branches of a tree.

Sydney pulled the shivering hedgehog out of the water.

"Oh, Sydney," wailed Taylor. "I did it again. I curled into a ball. I always do. I say I won't and then I do!"

"It's your nature," said Sydney, putting an arm around his friend. "You're a hedgehog, and a frightened hedgehog rolls up into a ball."

"I bet you fought off the dog," said Taylor. "I bet you were fierce and wild!"

"I gave her something to think about," said Sydney. "That's *my* nature. We are who we are, Taylor." He patted his friend, then looked around. "In the meantime, we're still lost."

As they began to walk back to the road, Taylor lifted his nose and sniffed.

"Do you smell it, Sydney?" he asked.

"I can't smell anything but me," said Sydney.

"I can!" shouted Taylor, hurrying toward the road. "I know that smell. It's Miss Nancy!"

Chapter 10

"And I know *that* smell," said Sydney. "It's a tuna fish sandwich!"

"It's coming from her car," said Taylor.

The two small animals watched from under a bush.

"There's a tuna fish sandwich in that car," said Sydney, "and I'm going to eat it."

"You can't get in Miss Nancy's car!" said Taylor.

Cars were loud and dangerous. They often hurt small animals.

"Oh yes I can," said Sydney. "It's an expedition! Plus, I'm really hungry."

He began to cross the road.

"Yipes!" said Taylor and he hurried to catch up with his brave, hungry friend.

Just then a loud truck came growling around a bend in the road. It was going very fast.

Sydney looked up.

Taylor looked up.

Miss Nancy looked up.

But it was too late.

Snap!

Taylor curled into a tight ball in the middle of the road.

And the truck kept coming, faster and faster.

Chapter 11

Stop!

If Sydney had known how to speak the words of humans, he would have shouted that word as loudly as he could.

But all he could do was stamp his feet and hiss in the middle of the road.

The truck kept coming, faster and faster.

Sydney stood by his friend.

"*Stop!*" shouted Miss Nancy.

She stepped into the middle of the road.

She waved a bunch of flowers at

the truck driver.

The truck slowed down.

"Are you in trouble?" called the truck driver.

"No," said Miss Nancy. "But you are driving very fast on a small road. And there are animals that cross here often."

Miss Nancy kept talking to the driver. Taylor and Sydney couldn't understand her human words.

"Taylor!" hissed Sydney. "GET UP!"

Taylor uncurled himself. "I did it again!"

"Follow me!" said Sydney.

Taylor and Sydney scrambled into the back of Miss Nancy's car.

A moment later, Miss Nancy got into the car. She put the flowers on the front seat.

"Wow!" she said. "That is some skunk smell."

She closed the door and drove home.

At her house, she left the car door open while she took the flowers inside.

Sydney and Taylor scampered to their burrow.

Miss Nancy came outside and closed the car door.

"I wonder what happened to my tuna fish sandwich?" said Miss Nancy.

She smiled and looked toward the potting shed.

Chapter 12

"The best expedition ever," said Sydney, collapsing into his armchair. "Promise me we'll never do it again."

"We'll see," said Taylor, returning the map of the Whole Wide World to the wall.

He traced his paw over the path of their journey.

They had gone to Places Unknown.

They had been wild animals.

They had battled ferocious predators.

Best of all, they had returned home.

"We should write a book about our great adventure," said Taylor, yawning. "We could be authors!"

"Authors," said Sydney, closing his eyes. "Wouldn't that be something?"

JACQUELINE DAVIES is the best-selling author of the Lemonade War series, which has inspired young readers across the world to raise money for charitable causes. Like Taylor, Jacqueline often gets Big Ideas and can't rest until she tries them out. These ideas have led her to live in Greece (where she bravely battled scorpions) and France (where she bravely battled French pastry). She has also explored more countries than she has fingers and toes. She loves to see the Whole Wide World, but, like Sydney, she also loves to return to her cozy burrow, which is currently just outside of Boston. Visit her online at jacquelinedavies.net.

DEBORAH HOCKING is the illustrator of several picture books, including the three titles in the Max Explains Everything series written by Stacy McAnulty. Like Taylor, Deborah loves adventure, which led her to spend seven years in Europe and Central America. She also accomplished her own expedition: an 1,100-mile hike across France and Spain. Deborah's current burrow is in Portland, Oregon, where she likes to escape the rain in cozy coffee shops, and explore wild places with her pup, Luna Lu, and husband, Jay. Visit her online at deborahhockingstudio.com and on Instagram @deborahhockingstudio.